Black Cat Goes Away

Written by Jill Eggleton

Illustrated by Chantal Stewart

Rigby

This is a
story about
Black Cat...

Black Cat

Mick...

Mick

and
Mrs. Finn.

Mrs. Finn

The place
in the book

Mick had a box for Mrs. Finn, so he stopped at her house. He went up to the door.

"This is for you," he said.

Black Cat ran up to the van.
The door was open,
so he jumped in.
He got under the boxes.

Mick came back.
He went down the road with the boxes and Black Cat.
He looked at his list.

"I have to stop here and here and here," he said.

Black Cat will...?

6

Mick stopped at the next house, but
Black Cat stayed in the van.
A big box was in the van, and
Black Cat went...

SCRATCH!

SCRATCH!

SCRATCH!

on the box with his claws.

The box came open, so Black Cat got inside.

Black Cat will...

go to sleep?

stay awake?

Mick came back.
He went down the road
to the next house.

"**The big box is for this house**,"
said Mick.

Mick got out the big box with
Black Cat inside.

A man came to the door.

"I have a big box for you," said Mick.

And he gave the man the box.

Black Cat's tail went up.
His hair went up.
His claws came out.
Black Cat went…

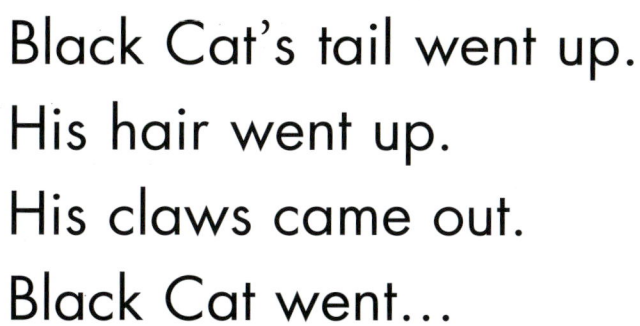

YEOWWWWWW!

and…

Black Cat jumped out of the box!

"**Help!**" said Mick.
"**Where did that cat come from?**"

"**It's not my cat,**"
said the man.
"**It can't stay here.**"

The man took the box.

"**You can have the cat,**"
he said.

What will Mick do with Black Cat?

Mick went back down the road with Black Cat.

He went back to all the houses.

But Black Cat's tail went up.

His hair went up.

His claws came out.

And he went...

YEOWWWWWW!

And all the people shouted...

"NO!
He's not my cat!"

Mick stopped at
Mrs. Finn's house.
He went up to the door
with Black Cat.

Mrs. Finn opened the door and Black Cat went…

YEOWWWWWW!

"This is my cat," said Mrs. Finn. "Where did you find him?"

"In a box," said Mick. "Your cat was in a box."

Mrs. Finn took Black Cat inside and shut the door.

"What will you do next?" she asked.

The End

Story sequence

Did the story go like this?

Did the story go like this?

Word Bank

box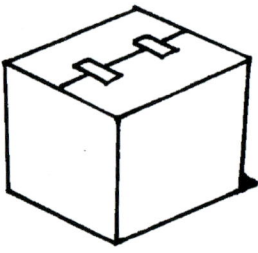

tail

claws

van

list